Seamore
the Starfish

Kristyn Fedich

Written by

Kristyn Fedich

Illustrated by

Hazel Quintanilla

ISBN: 1497454298 · ISBN 13: 9781497454293

Library of Congress Control Number: 2014906179

CreateSpace Independent Publishing Platform, North Charleston, SC

About the Author:

Kristyn Fedich is a first grade teacher and reading specialist in New Jersey. She lives with her husband and her Akita, Koby. Kristyn loves the beach and is inspired by the ocean and its animals. Her favorite sea animal is a starfish, which is where she got the inspiration for Seamore!

For more information about Seamore, visit www.seamorethestarfish.com

Seamore
the Starfish

Written by
Kristyn Fedich

Illustrated by
Hazel Quintanilla

Seamore the starfish lived on the ocean floor.

He lived in a cozy sand bed with his
Mom, Dad, and his little sister, Sally.

Seamore did not like the way he was shaped.

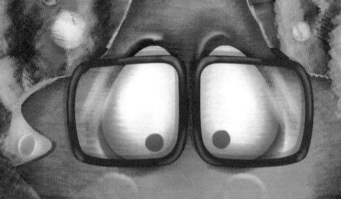

He was pointy and strange looking. Seamore could not fit in fun spots in the beautiful ocean like his other friends could.

When Seamore would play hide and seek with his friends Rayna and Eli, he could never find good places to hide because of his shape.

Hide and seek always ended with Seamore being it or trying to hide himself under the sand on the sparkling ocean floor.

Seamore just felt different and he felt he did not fit in well. He was sad.

Seamore's parents were worried. They tried to help Seamore.

"Is there anything at school you could join? Maybe a club or a sport with your friends, Rayna and Eli?" his mother asked.

"Maybe you could try football?
You would be great at that!"
his father suggested.

"I don't know," Seamore said quietly. "What if I am not good at football?"
"You can always try, and if it is not for you, that's ok, too!" his father replied with a smile.

Seamore was nervous, but he did like the idea of joining football with friends. He still worried, though.

"What if the other kids make fun of me? What if I trip on the field? What if the ball smacks me in the face?" Seamore thought nervously to himself.

The next day, Seamore talked to Rayna and Eli. "Wow! What a great idea, Seamore. You would be a great addition to our team," Rayna said excitedly.

"Yes, Seamore! That would be awesome! We would have so much fun together." Eli shouted.

Rayna, Eli, and Seamore went to football practice after school the next day. Rayna and Eli encouraged Seamore to jump in with the other kids. Seamore stepped out onto the field.

Seamore watched all the other kids practicing and playing. Some kids looked at him funny. One kid, Harry, said he was too odd shaped to play football.

Eli came over to Seamore. "Don't listen to Harry. He can be a bully sometimes. Go way out and try to catch the ball from me."

Eli swam back a bit and Seamore scooted further away. Eli threw the ball as hard as he could. Seamore's eyes became very big as the ball came straight at him.

"Oh no," thought Seamore. "I don't think I can do this."

With all eyes turned to him, Seamore leapt as high into the crystal blue water as he could.

SMACK! The ball was in between Seamore's arms. He had caught it! Seamore smiled a smile as big as the vast ocean.

All of the children swam over to him as fast as they could. They were all so excited for Seamore. Even Harry gave him a pat on the back.

Everyone was proud of Seamore for trying something new. Harry took Seamore aside and spoke softly, "Come play at our game on Saturday. We could really use you and your amazing arms!" Seamore's heart warmed and he was so proud of himself for coming out to try football with his friends.

After practice, Seamore rushed home to tell his parents all about his exhilarating time at football. He told them about the game on Saturday, and they all made plans to make a day of it together.

Saturday came and Seamore met Rayna, Eli, and their families at the Ocean Grove Park. "Remember Seamore, it is just a game. And it is just for fun," his mother said sweetly.

Seamore, Rayna, Eli, Harry, and all the other kids had a great game. Seamore scored two touchdowns. Even though their team lost, everyone ended the day with a smile.

As the team and their families headed to the Coral Cone for some ice cream after the game, Seamore's parents pulled him aside.

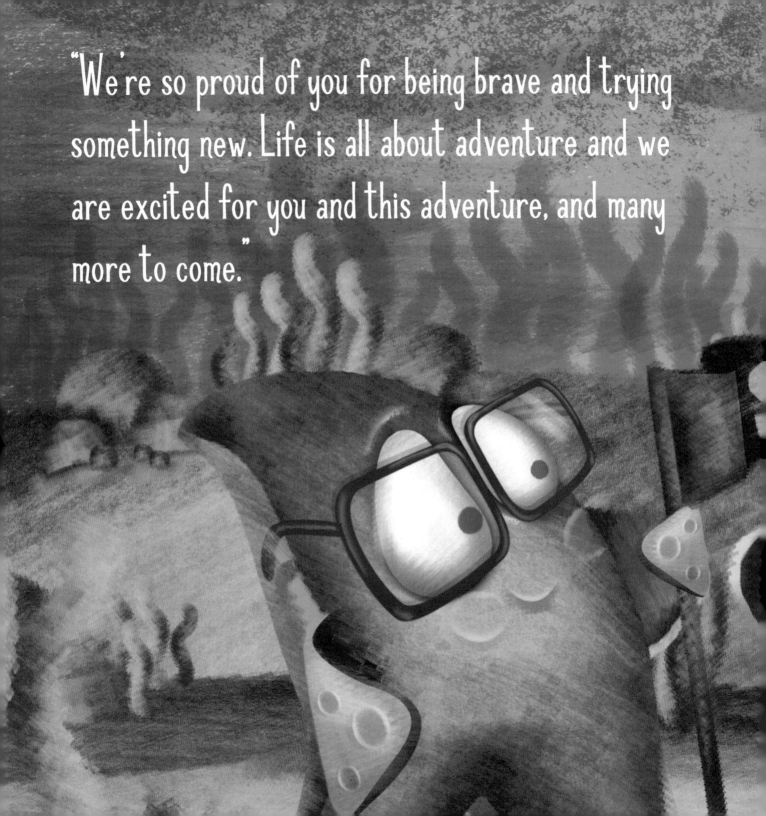

"We're so proud of you for being brave and trying something new. Life is all about adventure and we are excited for you and this adventure, and many more to come."

They all enjoyed their ice cream
and laughed the afternoon away.